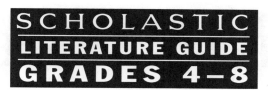

SCHOLASTIC
LITERATURE GUIDE
GRADES 4–8

Where the Red Fern Grows

by

Wilson Rawls

Written by Linda Ward Beech
Cover design by Vincent Ceci and Jaime Lucero
Interior design by Robert Dominguez and Jaime Lucero for Grafica, Inc.
Original cover and interior design by Drew Hires
Interior illustrations by Jenny Williams
Jacket cover from WHERE THE RED FERN GROWS by Wilson Rawls. Used by permission of Dell Books, a division of Bantam Doubleday Dell Publishing Group, Inc.

ISBN 0-590-37357-9
Copyright © 1997 by Scholastic, Inc.
All rights reserved.
Printed in the U.S.A.

JF Rawls

Where the red fern grows

MAY 19 '10

Table of Contents

Before Reading the Book

SUMMARY

At age 10 Billy Colman decides he must have two hound dogs. It takes him two years to save the money, but he finally has enough to order the dogs. He names his pups Little Ann and Old Dan. From then on, Billy and his dogs spend most nights hunting raccoons along the river bottom in the foothills of the Ozarks where he lives. As Billy becomes prouder and more attached to his dogs, it becomes clear that they are a unique team. Old Dan is a bold fighter, and Little Ann is as smart as they come. The dogs are intensely loyal to one another and to Billy. The story is packed with hair-raising hunting adventures and glorious moments of triumph. By the time Billy's grandpa enters the dogs in a championship coon hunt, they are known all over the county. Billy and his dogs win the contest, but not long afterward, they encounter a mountain lion while hunting. In killing the lion Old Dan becomes fatally injured. Little Ann dies soon after from grief, and Billy buries them both in a lovely spot on top of a hill. In the spring a beautiful red fern grows up between the graves. According to an old Indian legend, that spot would be forever sacred.

STORY CHARACTERS

People

Billy Colman . . . . Main character
Mama . . . . Billy's mother
Papa . . . . Billy's father
Grandpa . . . . Billy's grandfather
Stationmaster . . . . Kept Billy's dogs in Tahlequah
Marshal. . . . . Billy's friend in Tahlequah
Parker boys, Old Man Potter, Bufords,
Bill Lowery, Old Man Pritchard,
Mrs. Pritchard, Hatfords, Jim Hodges,
and Tom Logan . . . . Neighbors of the Colmans
Rubin Pritchard . . . . Neighbor and bully
Rainie Pritchard . . . . Rubin's younger brother
Mr. Kyle . . . . Owner of big walker hounds
Dr. Charley Lathman . . . . Owner of black and tan hounds
Mr. Benson . . . . Hunter who finds Billy's dogs

Animals

Buddie. . . . . Old red hound
Samie . . . . Colmans' cat
Daisy . . . . Colmans' milk cow
Sloppy Ann . . . . Colmans' hog
Big Dan. . . . . Billy's hound
Little Ann . . . . Billy's hound

ABOUT THE AUTHOR

Like the main character in his book, Wilson Rawls spent his boyhood on a small farm in the Oklahoma Ozarks in the heart of the Cherokee nation. He explored the hills and river bottoms with his dog, a bluetick hound, and it was to this dog that Rawls told his first stories. It wasn't until his family moved to Muskogee and Rawls attended high school, that he encountered books. *Where the Red Fern Grows*, set in Rawls' childhood homeland, became a classic in young adult literature.

LITERATURE CONNECTIONS

Other famous dog stories include:
- *Shiloh* by Phyllis Reynolds Naylor
- *Lassie Come Home* by Eric Knight
- *Old Yeller* by Fred Gipson
- *Sounder* by William H. Armstrong
- *Dogsong* by Gary Paulsen
- *White Fang* by Jack London
- *Ginger Pye* by Eleanor Estes

VOCABULARY

The following words are used in the book and may be unfamiliar to students. You might assign several words to each student. Have students look up their words and be prepared to present them to the class on a predetermined Word Celebration Day. Encourage students to be creative in their presentations. In addition to giving definitions, parts of speech, inflected forms, and sample sentences, students might make posters, banners, or wallet cards with their words. They might also plan to illustrate their words with photos, drawings, or skits. Remind students to look for these words as they read the book.

residential	cur	rind	whimper
quench	caress	allotted	aromatic
squall	canebrake	festered	mulled
heft	urgency	work-calloused	riffle
depot	sorghum	hillbilly	muster
britches	anvil	aggressive	ventured
vicious	romping	trance	querying
obstacle	wily	gouge	leverage
persistence	limber	rodent	domain
cinch	liniment	momentum	nonchalantly
spellbound	belligerent	bewildered	runt
slough	hysterical	shinnying	predicament
cunning	fatal	flinty	eddy
trough	dauber	bootlegger	smirked

disposition	begrudgingly	designated	maneuver
surpassed	taut	protruding	jubilant
gloating	monotonous	eerie	pruned
doused	lull	haggard	squabble
predatory	berserk	lithe	decipher

NOTES ABOUT FICTION

Although *Where the Red Fern Grows* is fiction, students can learn a lot about a way of life of a group of people; in this case, poor farmers in the Ozarks several decades ago. You may wish to point out that hunting raccoons was more than a sport for Billy and his neighbors; it was also a way to earn money. Billy sold the skins to help out his family. As students read the story, have them note how their lives differ from that of Billy. You may wish to make a Venn diagram that students can add to as they learn new information.

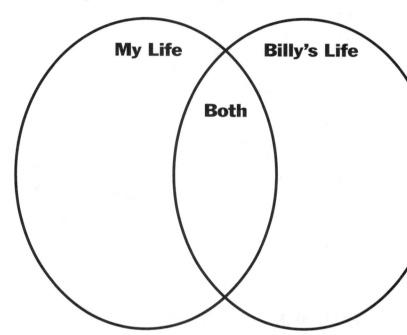

GETTING STARTED

As you preview the book with the class, you might draw students' attention to the following:

• *Title*—Ask students to guess what the title means. Have them record their ideas and check them later when they have finished reading the story. Ask: What is a red fern? Why is where it grows important?

• *Cover*—Discuss the illustration on the front cover. What are the boy and dogs looking at? Why is it night?

TEACHER TIP

A good way to keep in touch with students as they read is to use response journals. In a response journal, the pages are divided in half vertically. Students write questions and responses in their journals after each reading assignment. They then give the journals to you or a partner who responds to their comments in the second column

Exploring the Book

CHAPTERS 1 – 7

WHAT HAPPENS

As the story opens, a man sees some dogs fighting in an alley. His eye is caught by a fierce old redbone hound that the others are attacking. The man takes the dog home and feeds and cleans him; memories of other dogs from his boyhood come flooding back . . .

Billy has his heart set on a pair of coon hounds. In a discarded magazine he finds an ad for redbone pups—just what he wants. For the next two years Billy works hard and saves his pennies until he has enough for the dogs. With the help of his grandfather, he sends in his order. The pups arrive at the depot in the town of Tahlequah, and Billy sets out by foot to get them. When a gang of kids attacks Billy and his pups, he fights hard and is befriended by the town marshal. On the way home Billy and his pups hear a mountain lion. Billy names the pups Old Dan and Little Ann; he introduces them to his surprised family. He begins to train the hound dogs to hunt raccoons.

QUESTIONS TO TALK ABOUT
COMPREHENSION AND RECALL

1. Why does Grandpa say that Billy shouldn't tell his father about the dogs? (*His father wants to buy a mule and probably could use the money Billy is saving.*)

2. Why do the names carved in the tree seem perfect to Billy for his pups? (*They are in the clearing where Billy found the magazine ad, the same clearing where he prayed for pups.*)

3. Why do Billy's parents think they should move to town? (*They want the children to go to school and be exposed to the world.*)

4. How do the curiosity and stubbornness of a raccoon enable Billy to trap one? (*The trap lures the curious coon with something shiny. Because the raccoon is stubborn, it won't let go of the shiny item and its paw gets stuck.*)

HIGHER LEVEL THINKING SKILLS

5. Why is Grandpa dumbfounded when Billy brings in his $50? (*He probably didn't realize how serious Billy was or think he could save so much money.*)

6. Why doesn't Billy tell his parents he is going to Tahlequah? (*They don't know about the dogs; he is afraid to tell them.*)

7. How is Billy's life different from that of the children in town? (*He doesn't wear shoes, is schooled at home; spends his time by the river and in the mountains.*)

8. Why do Billy and his father care about whether a raccoon is caught in a sportsmanlike way? (*Part of the hunt is outwitting the clever raccoon; they have respect for the animal.*)

LITERARY ELEMENTS

9. Character revelation: What does it show about Billy's character when he buys gifts for his family? (*He is a thoughtful boy; he cares about his family and doesn't mean to upset them.*)

10. Foreshadowing: Who is the man in the first chapter? Why does the author start the story that way? (*The man is Billy. Although he never went back to the Ozarks, his memories and respect for hounds never left him. The author wants the reader to understand how important this time was in Billy's life.*)

PERSONAL RESPONSE

11. What things would you be willing to wait and work for for two years?

CROSS-CURRICULAR ACTIVITIES

LANGUAGE ARTS: *Look at the Language*
As students read the book, draw their attention to the way Wilson Rawls uses language. For instance, you might point out the colorful verbs he uses. Give as examples:

- "river was <u>studded</u> with tall sycamore"
- "the dogs <u>boiled</u> out of an alley"
- "he <u>scooted</u> under the barn"
- "squirrel <u>barked</u> a warning"
- "out of the pipe <u>spurted</u> a boy"

Ask students to find at least five or ten more interesting uses of verbs in the story to share with the class. Point out that good writers select their verbs carefully and avoid overused words.

SOCIAL STUDIES: *Seeing the Setting*
Remind students that the story takes place in the Ozarks of northeastern Oklahoma. Ask students to read for descriptions of the Ozarks in the story, and then to do further research to extend their knowledge of these mountains. Assign the reproducible map on page 16 to help students locate the Ozarks.

SCIENCE: *Hound Dogs*
Several kinds of hounds are mentioned in the book including redbones, blueticks, walkers, and blood hounds. Hounds hunt by either sight or scent; many such as those in the story, bay when they locate their game. Animal fans will enjoy reading up on hounds and preparing fact sheets for the class. Encourage students to illustrate their material.

WHAT HAPPENS

Billy begins hunting with his dogs. On the first hunt of the season, the dogs tree a raccoon up a huge sycamore. The only way Billy can get it out is to chop down the tree which takes him several days. One night during the winter, Little Ann slips into icy waters and can't get out by herself. Big Dan quits the hunt and goes to help her. Billy risks his own life pulling her from the river. As the fame of Billy's dogs spreads, the Pritchard boys challenge him, saying that Little Ann and Big Dan can't tree the ghost coon. Although Billy doesn't want to bet, Grandpa calls the bet. The three boys take the dogs out, but when the coon is treed, Billy doesn't want it killed. Rubin Pritchard accidentally falls on an ax and is fatally injured. Billy feels bad and secretly lays flowers on his grave. Grandpa tells Billy about a championship coon hunt in which he has entered Big Dan and Little Ann.

QUESTIONS TO TALK ABOUT

COMPREHENSION AND RECALL

1. Why does Mama worry about Billy? (*He is out alone at night hunting; she is afraid harm will come to him.*)

2. How does Papa's treatment of Billy change? (*He begins to treat him like a man—with more respect.*)

3. Why doesn't Billy give up when his dogs have a raccoon up the "big tree"? (*He promised the dogs they'd get a raccoon.*)

4. How do the Pritchard boys get Billy to accept their bet? (*They insult Grandpa who gets mad and puts up the money.*)

HIGHER LEVEL THINKING SKILLS

5. Why would a hunter respect raccoons? (*They are very clever at misleading dogs; they put up a good fight—a challenge.*)

6. Why does Grandpa put soap in Billy's pocket? (*He is "washing his mouth out with soap" when Billy's stories get too far-fetched.*)

7. Why does Grandpa lock the store when he goes to the mill? (*He doesn't trust the Pritchard boys.*)

8. Do miracles really happen to Billy, or does he solve his own problems? (*Answers will vary; students should give reasons.*)

9. Why doesn't Billy want to kill the ghost coon? (*He has too much respect for him.*)

10. Would Rubin have killed Billy's dogs if he hadn't tripped on the ax? Give reasons for your answer. (*Possible: Yes, he was proud of his dog and thought it might be killed by Billy's dogs. He wasn't afraid of violence. No, he might hit his own dog by mistake.*)

LITERARY ELEMENTS

11. Narrative suspense: Why doesn't the author tell what Billy's father is doing with the money Billy earns? (*Possible: It's not important to the story. Or, he doesn't want to give the ending away.*)

12. Characterization: What does Billy's treatment of Rubin tell you about Billy? (*He isn't mean like Rubin; he believes in a fair contest.*)

PERSONAL RESPONSE

13. Which of Billy's dogs would you like to have? Why?

14. How did you feel about Grandpa accepting the Pritchards' bet?

CROSS-CURRICULAR ACTIVITIES

SOCIAL STUDIES: *Names from Nature*

Pea Vine Hollow, Sparrow Hawk Mountain, Bluebird Creek. . .these are some of the colorful place names in *Where the Red Fern Grows*. Point out that these names describe wildlife in the area. Have students work in groups and study maps for states sharing the Ozark Plateau such as Oklahoma, Missouri, and Arkansas. Ask each group to come up with a list of place names that

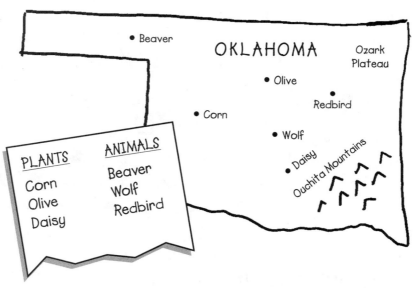

describe plants or animals. Have students create large maps on which these places are located. Display the maps in the classroom.

WRITING: *Yes or No?*

Have students write short essays that address these questions: In what way(s) did Billy win the bet with the Pritchards? In what way(s) did he lose it? Call on volunteers to read aloud their essays, then lead a class discussion on the issues.

WHAT HAPPENS

Billy, Grandpa, Papa, and the dogs attend the championship coon hunt. Little Ann wins the contest for the best-looking hound. The dogs do well on their hunt and qualify for the runoff. During the final hunt, there is a bad sleet storm. Old Dan gets lost, and Grandpa is injured. The party suffers through the night in a gully, but Billy's dogs come through and win the contest. Billy gets a box of money and a gold cup. Back home again, Grandpa gets good care, and Billy continues to hunt. One night he and the dogs meet up with a mountain lion, and Old Dan challenges the big cat. After a horrible fight, Old Dan is mortally wounded and the mountain lion is dead. A few days later, Little Ann dies of grief. Billy buries the dogs on top of a hill. Papa tells Billy that with the money Billy has earned, the family can move to town. Just before they leave, Billy finds the red fern growing over the two graves. He recalls that according to an Indian legend, a spot is sacred where the red fern grows.

QUESTIONS TO TALK ABOUT
COMPREHENSION AND RECALL

1. Why are Billy's dogs unusual? (*They fight together, won't eat until the other one does, save one another from danger, share food, watch over Billy.*) You might have students complete the reproducible on page 15 after they answer this question.

2. How does Big Dan's behavior get Billy and the dogs in trouble? (*He challenges any game which often leads to difficult situations. He fights the mountain lion.*)

3. Why does Billy bury Old Dan on the hillside? (*He would be able to hear hounds as they hunted through the countryside; it was a beautiful spot.*)

HIGHER LEVEL THINKING SKILLS

4. Why do the hunters at the contest treat Billy like an equal? (*They respect his dogs and are good sportsmen.*)

5. Did Grandpa sign up for the contest for Billy's sake or his own sake? (*Answers will vary. Students should give reasons.*)

6. How do you know that Billy is a good hunter? (*He uses his experience; is patient; knows his dogs well; is a good judge of the habits of raccoons.*)

7. Why is Billy so willing to give his cup to his youngest sister? (*She asks for it; he loves her; it is enough for him to win the contest.*)

8. How is Billy helped to understand his dogs' deaths? (*The legend of the red fern helps him.*)

LITERARY ELEMENTS

9. Foreshadowing: On the way to the contest, Billy hears two screech owls—a sign of bad luck. How does this event foreshadow events in the story? (*His dogs both die not long afterward.*)

PERSONAL RESPONSE

10. Does Billy needlessly expose himself and others to danger during the storm?

11. Mama says, "Everyone needs help some time in his life." Describe a time when you really needed help.

12. Did you like the book? Why or why not?

CROSS-CURRICULAR ACTIVITIES

READING: *Back to the Beginning*
Recall with students how the book begins, then ask them to go back and reread the first chapter. Discuss: Who is the man in this chapter? How are the cups like Old Dan and Little Ann? Why do you think Billy never went back to his childhood home? Why does the author begin the book this way?

LANGUAGE ARTS: *Legends*
Review the legend of the red fern with students. Point out that there are many legends involving plants. Perhaps students are familiar with *The Legend of the Indian Paintbrush* by Tomie dePaola. Encourage students to learn a legend to retell to the class. Set aside a storytelling hour for students' legends.

ART: *Through a Reader's Eyes*
Most readers visualize scenes and characters as they read a book. Ask students to share their visualizations with the class by drawing or painting a favorite scene from *Where the Red Fern Grows.* Plan an art exhibit to display the finished work.

Summarizing the Book

PUTTING IT ALL TOGETHER

You can choose from the following activities to help students summarize and review *Where the Red Fern Grows.*

CLASS PROJECT: *Literary Categories*

Write the headings CHARACTER, SETTING, EVENTS on the chalkboard. Then assign each student to one of the categories. Explain that students are to make up a question about the book for their category. For example, a student in the Character group might ask: Who was the most helpful to Billy in getting his dogs? (*Grandpa*) Review the questions and work with any students who need to revise theirs. Then have students write their questions on an index card and identify the category on the back of the card. Make a master list of the questions and answers. Mix up the cards and place them face down in a pile. Have students divide into teams. Each team takes turns sending a member up to pick a question, identify the category to the class, and then answer the question. If a question is not answered correctly, the other team gets a chance.

Character	Setting	Events
Who was the most helpful to Billy in getting his dogs? (Grandpa)		

GROUP PROJECT: *Roundtable Discussions*

Assign students to work in groups. Ask each group to come up with a list of open-ended discussion questions about the book. You might also suggest some of the questions in this guide. Select one or two questions for each group, then have students meet at a round table to discuss them. Beforehand, have the groups set some guidelines. For example:

- There are no right or wrong answers; the point is to explore the material.
- Each group should have a leader who calls on others to participate.
- Everyone is responsible for contributing to the discussion.

INDIVIDUAL PROJECT: *Story Trees*
Have students draw a tree such as the one shown here. Then give them a list of items to fill in on each line. For example: 1. Character's name. 2. Description of character. 3. Description of setting. 4. What the character wants. 5. Description of an exciting event involving the character.

EVALUATION IDEAS
You might use the following rubric to assess students' work on the Story Tree.
• Did the student follow the directions for each line correctly?
• Did the student demonstrate an understanding of the character. setting, and events?
• Did the student choose descriptive words carefully?

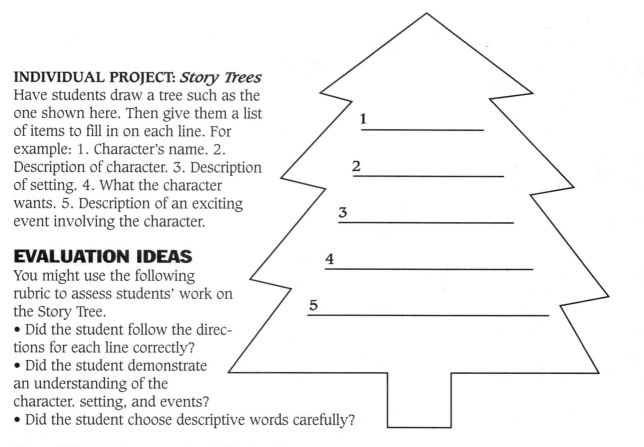

Possible Answers for Worksheets
page 14: Answers will vary, but students should use the type of word or clause indicated.
page 15: Possible: Little Ann—sweet, small and delicate, very smart, patient, runt of the litter, playful, beautiful; Old Dan—bold, tough, heavy, solid, aggressive, unpredictable, stubborn, impatient, foolish; Both—loyal, good hunter, brave, unusual.
page 16: 1. northeast 2. Check to see that students circle Tahlequah. 3. Illinois River 4. Oklahoma City; west 5. Colorado, Texas, Arkansas, Missouri, New Mexico, and Kansas; Arkansas

Book Libs

Fill in each blank with the type of word or words suggested.

If you want to read a _____ book, try *Where the Red Fern Grows*
                          adjective

by _____. This story is about a _____ boy
              author   adjective

named _____ and his two _____ dogs. Parts of the
            proper noun   adjective

book are very _____ because _____
                    adjective   independent clause

_____.

Other parts of the story are very _____
                                                    adjective

because_____.
                          independent clause

Reading this book made me feel _____. I think the author
                                              adjective

wrote this book so that _____
                                      independent clause

_____

_____

_____

_____.

Name: _____

Billy's Team

Little Ann and Old Dan are very different dogs, but they make a great team. Decide which of the words and phrases describe each dog and write them under the correct heading in the diagram. If a word describes both dogs, write it in the middle.

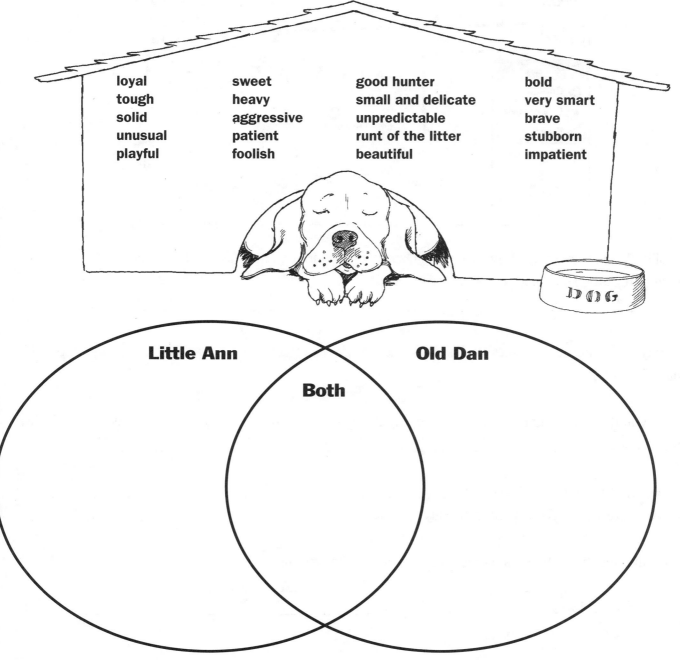

loyal
tough
solid
unusual
playful

sweet
heavy
aggressive
patient
foolish

good hunter
small and delicate
unpredictable
runt of the litter
beautiful

bold
very smart
brave
stubborn
impatient

Little Ann

Both

Old Dan

In the Ozarks

The setting for *Where the Red Fern Grows* is in the Ozarks of Oklahoma. Use the map to answer the questions.

Name: _____

1. Billy Colman and his family live in the Ozarks of Oklahoma. Find the Ozark Plateau on the map. In what part of the state is it?

_____

2. Billy walks 20 miles to pick up his dogs at the depot in Tahlequah. Find and circle Tahlequah on the map.

3. Billy and his dogs do much of their hunting along a river. What is the river near Tahlequah that Billy hunts along? _____

4. What is the capital of Oklahoma? _____
In what direction is the capital from Billy's home? _____

5. Oklahoma shares borders with six other states. What are they?

_____

Which state is closest to Billy's home? _____